Every new generation of children is enthralled by the famous stories in our Well Loved Tales series. Younger ones love to have the story read to them. Older children will enjoy the exciting stories in an easy-to-read text.

Revised edition

Published by Ladybird Books Ltd Loughborough Leicestershire UK
Ladybird Books Inc Auburn Maine 04210 USA

Printed in England (7)

Jack and the Beanstalk

retold for easy reading
by VERA SOUTHGATE, M A B Com

illustrated by MARTIN SALISBURY

Ladybird Books

JACK AND THE BEANSTALK

Once upon a time there was a widow who had only one son, named Jack. He was a lazy boy. He would not go out to work for his living, nor would he do much work for his mother at home.

Yet Jack was not altogether a bad boy. He was kindhearted and pleasant and his mother was very fond of him.

Jack and his mother lived in a tiny cottage and they were very poor. As time went on, the widow grew poorer and poorer, while Jack grew lazier and lazier.

At last the day arrived when the widow had nothing left in the world, except one cow. Then she said to her son, "Tomorrow you must take our poor cow to market and sell her. She is all we have left in the world, so be sure that you get a good price for her."

Next morning Jack got up early and set off for market, with the cow. On the road he met a butcher who asked him where he was going with the cow.

"I'm taking her to market, to sell her, sir," Jack told him.

"I will make a bargain with you," said the butcher to Jack. "I will exchange these beans for your cow." He showed Jack some strange-looking beans, all of different colours, which he was carrying in his hat.

"I would be a fool to exchange my cow for your beans," said Jack.

"Ah, but these are not ordinary beans!" replied the butcher. "They are magic beans."

Jack thought what a fine thing it would be to have some magic beans, so he agreed to the bargain. He gave the cow to the butcher, put the beans in his pocket and set off for home.

Jack's mother was surprised to see him back so early. She thought he must have got a fine price for the cow.

"Look, mother!" cried Jack. "I have made a good bargain. I have exchanged our cow for these beans."

His mother was very, very angry. "You bad, stupid boy," she said, "now we shall surely starve." In her anger, she threw the beans out of the window and pushed Jack upstairs to bed, without any supper.

"But they are magic beans!" wailed Jack. "So I thought it was a good bargain." His mother was too angry to reply.

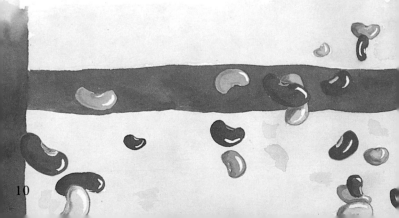

The next morning Jack woke early feeling very hungry. His room was much darker than usual. When he went to his window, he found he could hardly see out. There seemed to be a large tree in the garden where none had grown before.

Jack ran downstairs and discovered that it was not a tree that was growing in the garden, but a huge beanstalk. It had sprung up, during the night, from the magic beans that his mother had thrown out of the window. The beanstalk was taller and stronger than any tree, and it had grown so quickly that its top was out of sight.

Jack began immediately to climb the beanstalk. It was hard work, pulling himself upwards from branch to branch, but Jack was a strong boy and he was determined to reach the top.

Jack climbed and he climbed and he climbed, yet whenever he looked up, the top of the beanstalk still stretched upwards, out of sight. And all the time he grew hungrier and hungrier.

At length, after many hours of climbing, Jack reached the top of the beanstalk and stepped off into a wild, bare country. Not a tree nor a blade of grass was to be seen and there was not a house in sight. A long road led away into the distance.

Jack set off along the road and soon he met an old, old woman.

"Good morning, Jack," she said, and Jack was amazed that she knew his name.

"I know all about you," said the old woman. "You are now in a country belonging to a wicked ogre. When you were a baby, this ogre killed your father and stole all that he possessed. That

is why your mother is now so poor. You must try to punish this ogre and get back your father's wealth," she continued. "If you are a brave boy, I shall try to help you."

At that the old woman disappeared and Jack went forward along the lonely road.

Towards evening Jack came to a castle. He knocked on the great door and a woman opened it. She looked startled when she saw Jack.

"I am very tired and hungry," said Jack, "please can you give me some supper and a bed for the night?"

"Oh! My poor boy!" cried the woman. "Do you not know where you are? My husband is an ogre and he eats people. He would be sure to find you and eat you for his supper."

Jack felt afraid when he heard this, but he was too tired and hungry to go another step, so he pleaded with the woman to take him in.

At last the ogre's wife agreed and she led Jack into her kitchen. There she set a fine supper before him, which Jack enjoyed so much that he soon forgot his fears.

Scarcely had he finished eating, when the ground was shaken by the sound of heavy, stamping feet. Then three loud knocks were heard on the door. It was the ogre returning home.

Jack's heart began to thump. The ogre's wife began to shake. She snatched Jack up and pushed him into the oven, which fortunately was nearly cold. Then she went to let her husband in.

The ogre stalked into the castle, sniffed round the kitchen and roared:

"Fee, fi, fo, fum,
I smell the blood of an Englishman,
Be he alive, or be he dead,
I'll grind his bones to make my bread."

"Nonsense!" said the ogre's wife, "you are dreaming," and she set an enormous meal on the table before him. As the ogre was hungry he sniffed no more but sat down and began to eat.

Jack peeped at the ogre through a crack in the oven door. He was astonished to see how much the ogre ate and how quickly he pushed the food into his mouth.

When the ogre had finished his meal, he shouted to his wife, "Bring me my hen." She brought it to him and he sent her off to bed, without a word of thanks.

Then the ogre placed the hen on the table and shouted "Lay," whereupon the hen laid a golden egg.

"Another!" roared the ogre, and another golden egg was laid.

Again and again, in a voice of thunder, the ogre shouted "Lay," and the hen obeyed, until twelve golden eggs were on the table. Then the ogre fell asleep in his chair and he snored so loudly that the castle shook.

As soon as Jack heard the snores of the ogre, he crept out of the oven. He seized the hen, tucked it under his arm and tiptoed out of the castle.

Then he set off running along the road, as fast as ever he could. On and on he ran, until at last he came to the top of the beanstalk. He climbed down quickly and took the wonderful hen to his mother.

She, poor woman, was delighted to see her son again. And, when Jack set the hen on the table and ordered it to lay a golden egg, she could not believe her eyes.

Every day the hen laid another golden egg. By selling the eggs, Jack and his mother were able to live very comfortably and had no need to worry. They lived happily in this way for many a long day.

But, after some time, Jack began to long for more adventure. He thought of what the old woman had told him and of how the ogre had stolen all his father's riches.

Jack determined to visit the ogre's castle again. He disguised himself so that the ogre's wife would not know him. Then he began to climb the beanstalk, for the second time.

Just as before, Jack reached the castle towards evening and knocked on the door. When the ogre's wife opened the door, he said, "I should be glad of food and rest, good woman, for I am hungry and tired."

"You cannot stay here," replied the ogre's wife. "Once before I took in a tired and hungry boy and he stole my husband's wonderful hen."

Jack pretended to think that the boy who had stolen the hen was a rascal. He chatted so pleasantly to the ogre's wife that she felt she could not refuse him a meal. She let him come in.

After Jack had eaten a good supper, the ogre's wife hid him in a cupboard. She had just done so, when in stamped the ogre. He sniffed all round the kitchen and roared:

"Fee, fi, fo, fum,
I smell the blood of an Englishman,
Be he alive, or be he dead,
I'll grind his bones to make my bread."

"Nonsense!" said the ogre's wife, "you are dreaming," and she set an enormous supper before him.

After supper the ogre roared, "Fetch me my

money bags.'' His wife brought the bags and went off to bed.

The ogre emptied all the money on to the table, and counted it over and over again before putting it back into the bags. Then he fell asleep.

As soon as Jack heard the ogre's loud snores, he crept out of the cupboard and picked up the money bags. They were much heavier than he had expected, but he managed to sling them over his shoulder. Then he let himself out of the castle as quietly as possible.

Jack could not run along the road because the money bags were so heavy. He was afraid that the ogre would waken and follow him, but he reached the top of the beanstalk safely.

Once more Jack's mother was overjoyed to see him, and when he emptied the money bags on to the table, she was astonished.

Jack and his mother now had all that they could wish for. With the money that Jack had brought from the ogre's castle, they built a bigger house and bought furniture, fine clothes and food.

The widow said to her son, "Now that we are rich, I beg you not to venture up the beanstalk again." But Jack would not promise this.

For a long time, Jack and his mother were well content. Then Jack began to long for more adventure and to think that the giant had not yet been punished enough. He determined to visit the ogre's castle once more.

This time Jack used another different disguise. He hoped that the ogre's wife would not recognise him and that he would be able to persuade her to invite him into the castle.

Then, for the third time, Jack climbed the beanstalk, followed the same path and arrived at the castle door. The ogre's wife did not recognise him and he begged for a night's lodging.

"No, no!" she cried. "You cannot come in here. The last two tired boys whom I took in were thieves. One stole a wonderful hen and the other some money bags. No, no, you cannot come in."

Jack begged and begged and at last the ogre's wife took pity on him, asked him in and gave him some supper. Then she hid him in the copper in which she washed her clothes.

Soon the ogre came home and, sniffing round the kitchen, roared:

"Fee, fi, fo, fum,
I smell the blood of an Englishman,
Be he alive, or be he dead,
I'll grind his bones to make my bread."

"Nonsense!" said his wife. "You are dreaming," and she set an enormous supper before him.

After supper the ogre shouted, "Bring me my harp." The ogre's wife brought a beautiful golden harp and set it on the table before him. Then she went off to bed.

"Play," roared the ogre, and the harp began to play of its own accord. Jack had never heard such sweet music as it played. The harp continued to play until the ogre was almost asleep. Then he shouted "Stop," and the music ceased.

As soon as Jack heard the loud snores of the ogre, he jumped out of the copper and seized the harp. No sooner had he touched it, than the harp called out, "Master, master."

The ogre woke up in a fury, to see Jack making off with his harp. "You are the boy who stole my hen and my money bags," he bellowed.

The ogre was still drowsy with sleep and heavy with food and wine, so he was not as speedy as usual. Yet he staggered to his feet and set off after Jack.

Jack was terrified but he did not put the harp down. Slinging it over his shoulder, he ran for his life towards the beanstalk. And all the way along

the road, the harp continued to cry, "Master, master." Jack was too frightened and too short of breath even to think of saying "Stop" to it.

Looking over his shoulder, Jack saw the ogre striding after him. Then he ran as he had never run before in his life.

Jack reached the top of the beanstalk safely, but the ogre was close behind him.

He scrambled and slid down the beanstalk, shouting, "Mother, mother, bring me the axe quickly. The ogre's coming."

Then Jack's mother picked up her skirts and, running more quickly than she had run since she was a little girl, she brought her son the axe.

By then the ogre was climbing rapidly down the beanstalk. Jack swung the axe with all his strength, and gave one mighty blow at the beanstalk.

The beanstalk toppled down and there was a tremendous thud as the ogre was thrown headlong to the ground. He fell dead in Jack's garden and so big was he that he filled it from end to end.

Pointing to the ogre, Jack said to his mother, "He killed my father and robbed us of all our wealth."

At that moment, there appeared the old woman who had talked to Jack. She told them that she was really a fairy, but that she had lost her magic power and been unable to prevent the ogre killing Jack's father.

It was she who had made Jack take the magic beans in exchange for the cow. She had wanted him to climb the beanstalk, and she had led him to the ogre's castle and helped him there.

"Your troubles are now over," the fairy told Jack and his mother. "You will want for nothing and you will be happy as long as you live."

It happened as the fairy had said, and Jack and his mother lived happily ever after.